LOOK AND SEE WHAT GOD GAVE ME

by Sally Anne Conan

Pictures by Kathy Rogers

PAULIST PRESS
New York / Mahwah, N.J.

ISBN: 0-8091-6645-3

Published by Paulist Press
997 Macarthur Boulevard
Mahwah, New Jersey 07430

Printed and bound in the United States of America

LOOK AND SEE WHAT GOD GAVE ME

Lovingly dedicated to "Saint Rock,"
Little Peter Joseph Hyrcza

"Each one has a special gift from God."

1 Corinthians 7:7

God put pretty stripes on zebras.

God put little wings on birds.

God put spots on little pups.

I wonder what God gave to me?

God put shiny pearls in oysters.

God put waves upon the sea.

God put shells on little turtles.

I wonder what God gave to me?

God put sprinkly spouts on whales.

God gave possums hanging tails.

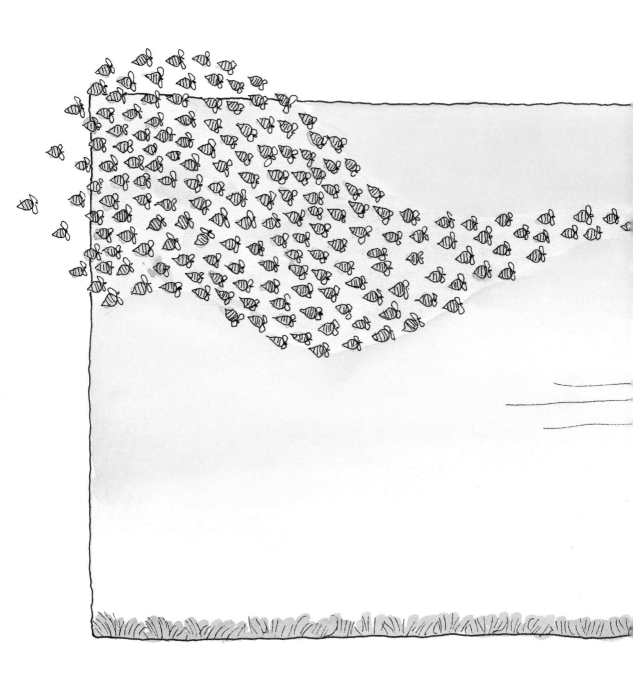

God put buzzes into bees.

I wonder what God gave to me?

I don't have stripes or spots or spouts.

My gift is hard to figure out!

You have to turn the page to see

The special gift God gave to me...

A SMILE!

Word List

a	I	pretty	tails
bees	into	pups	the
birds	is	put	turn
buzzes	little	sea	turtles
don't	me	see	upon
figure	my	shells	waves
gave	on	shiny	whales
gift	or	smile	what
God	out	special	wings
hanging	oysters	spots	wonder
hard	page	spouts	you
have	pearls	sprinkly	zebras
	possums	stripes	